This book is dedicated to our own
sisters, Pam and Lucy Kay.
Thank you for all your
support along the way!

In Memory of Hali

I Can Find a Way!

I'm Lucy Kay!

written by: Cheryl A. Cunningham, PE and Judith E. Cunningham, MEd
illustrated by: Jill M. VanMatre, BSc

PCS Engineers Publishing
1924 South Dan Jones Road
Avon, Indiana 46123
317-837-9900

Ordering information:
www.CreateSpace.com/5171322
www.amazon.com

Printed by CreateSpace, An Amazon.com Company

ISBN 978-0-9905344-1-9
Library of Congress Control Number: 2015932781

Book Layout and Design: Erin E. Güt
Fonts: Sassoon Primary, CurlzMT, Alegreya Sans Light, PWSimpleHandwriting, Noteworthy, Impact

The illustrations in this book were made with watercolor. For the "You Can Thanks to an Engineer," page, CAD was utilized to create illustrations and graph paper was used for the background.

First Edition, 2015

www.icanbeanengineer.com

Lucy Kay was SO excited.
Tomorrow was a very important day.
She was going to choose her song for the school
show! She knew she needed a good night's rest,
so she could do her very best.

She yawned an enormously gigantic yawn
and prepared her bed for sleeping.
"Kiki Cat, Henry Hog,
Chester Chicken, and Polywog Frog.
Comfy, cozy in my bed.
Love you all, you sleepyheads."

Then she snuggled in deep and whispered so sweet,
"Lay here quietly, not a peep.
It's time for us all to go to sleep."

"Goodnight, sleepy girl,"
said Mom.
"Goodnight, Doodle-Bug,"
said Dad.
"Nighty night,"
yawned Lucy Kay.

"Sleep tight, see you in the
morning light," whispered Mom
and Dad together.

Lucy Kay went right to sleep.

But right in the middle of her snoozing and her snoring, Lucy Kay sat straight up in bed, wide awake! "What is that noise?!" she whined.

That noise was her new baby sister in the room next door. She was hungry again and crying for more.

"Wah, wah, wah, wah, wah!" was all she could say.

Lucy Kay was very sorry that her new baby sister was crying,
but she really needed to go to sleep.

"Kiki Cat, Henry Hog, Chester Chicken, and Polywog Frog.
Comfy, cozy in my bed.
Love you all, you sleepyheads."

"Lay here quietly, not a peep.
It's time for us all to go to sleep."

She put her hands on her ears to block out the sound of crying
and drifted back to sleep.

But right in the middle of her
snoozing and her snoring, Lucy Kay
sat straight up in bed, wide awake!

"She's crying again?!" she said to herself.
"I covered my ears, and it blocked the sound,
but I can't seem to keep my hands on my ears when I'm asleep."

"Wah, wah, wah, wah, wah!" was all Lucy Kay could hear.

Lucy Kay scratched her head and looked around her bedroom.
"There must be something to keep the sound away."
She searched and searched until she found a few items she
thought just might do the trick.

Yawning an
enormously gigantic yawn,
Lucy Kay mumbled,
"Cat...Hog...Chicken...Frog.
Please go to sleep,
I'm as tired as a dog."

The next day was not a good day at school. Lucy Kay could barely stay awake. She almost fell asleep trying out songs for the school show.

She did fall asleep in Reading.

And at
Recess.

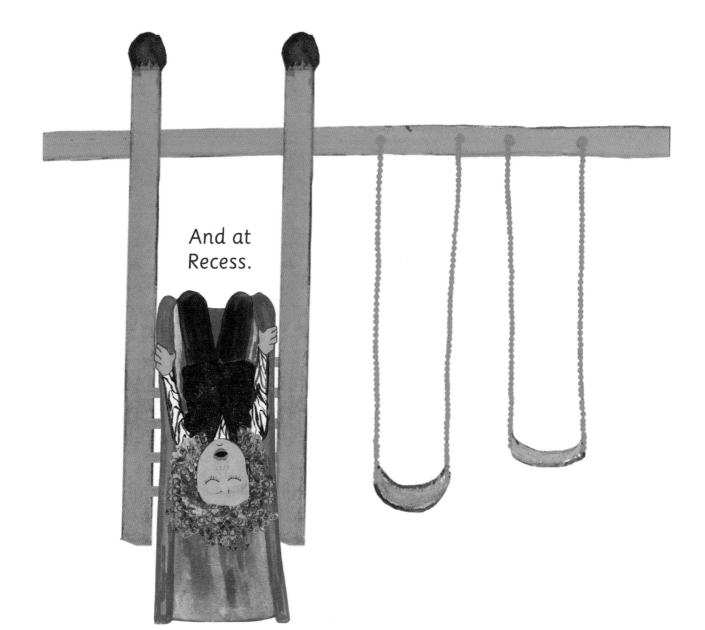

And even in her lunch.

Lucy Kay's teacher was very concerned.

That night while Lucy Kay got ready for bed, she thought about her problem. "I need to cover my ears with something that won't fall off when I go to sleep."

Suddenly she remembered her earmuffs!
"They stay on my head very nicely when I play outside. They should do the trick."

She put on her earmuffs and went right to sleep.
And slept...

And slept.

She slept right through her new
baby sister crying.

AND...

she slept right through
her alarm clock.

The next morning Lucy Kay woke
up to the beautiful sun shining
through her window.

And to her mom's very
loud voice.

"LUCY KAY!

Time to get up!

Right now!

You overslept!

You missed the bus!"

As soon as Lucy Kay
got to school, she knew
right away it was not
going to be a good day,
again.

Lucy Kay was very late.

She missed practicing songs
for the school show.
She missed Reading.
And Recess.
And she missed her lunch.

Lucy Kay's teacher was very concerned.

"Lucy Kay," said her teacher. "I know how a new baby sister sometimes cries during the night. It can be difficult for you, but I'm sure you will figure it out. When you have a problem to solve you never give up!"

Lucy Kay contemplated her predicament.

"The earmuffs worked great keeping the sound out of my ears,"
she thought to herself. "But it was also a problem.
I couldn't hear anything including my alarm clock.
But if I don't cover my ears,
the loud crying keeps waking me up.
I wish I could just put earmuffs on my wall!"

Suddenly, the most amazing idea popped right into her head!

Bursting through the front door, Lucy Kay exclaimed,

"I have the most amazing idea! May I borrow 3 blankets, 6 nails, 1 hammer, and may I have some assistance in my room?"

"Yes, yes, yes, and of course." said Mom and Dad hesitantly at the same time. "What are you constructing?"

"Giant earmuffs!" answered Lucy Kay.
Looking perplexed, Mom said "Giant earmuffs?"

"Yes," explained Lucy Kay, "I had a problem staying asleep when my new baby sister cried. I covered my ears to keep the sound out, but everything I put on my ears fell right off, so I kept waking up. Then I thought of earmuffs. They stayed on my ears all night, but they blocked ALL the sounds.

I didn't even hear my alarm clock and I was late for school. So I think if I put giant earmuffs on my wall, the sound will not get into my room."

"I really like the way you're thinking about different solutions to solve your problem," marveled Dad.

"This is magnificent!"
admired Lucy Kay.
"I can't wait to go to bed!"

The next morning Lucy Kay woke up to the beautiful sun shining through her window and to the sound of her alarm clock.

"Did my baby sister cry last night?" she asked.
"Yes, she did, Lucy Kay." answered Dad. "She woke up several times."

"It worked!! The giant earmuffs blocked the sound coming through my
wall! When I closed my eyes, I went right to sleep.
I didn't even hear a peep. "

"Lucy Kay, you found a way! We're so proud of you, my dear. You
solved your problem, just like an engineer!" praised Mom and Dad.

"An engineer?" asked Lucy Kay. "What do you mean, an engineer?"

"Engineers dream, imagine, design and create.
That's what makes their job so great.
They figure out ways of blocking sound,
so it can be quiet all around."

"Wow!" shouted Lucy Kay. "That sounds like fun.
I can do all those things, I want to be one!"

Now Lucy Kay was ready to sing in the school show.

She grabbed the microphone and was ready to go.

Oh I can dream,
imagine,
design, and create
And I
know how
to do something great!

Oh I can dream,
imagine,
design, and create
And I
know I
can do something great!

Oh yes I can
Oh yes I can
I'll find a way,
I'm Lucy Kay!

Oh yes I can,
Oh yes I can,
I'll find a way,
I'm Lucy Kay!

The audience
clapped and cheered
and shouted hurray,
but Lucy Kay
hushed the crowd.
She had
something to say.

"This
announcement is
for the whole
world to hear!"

"I'm going to be an Engineer!"

Our Team

An Engineer, a Teacher, and an Artist

Sisters, Cheryl and Judy Cunningham, share a passion
for positively influencing children and youth.

As a professional engineer, Cheryl (the engineer) wanted
to introduce the fun and excitement of engineering by
demonstrating that problem solving in everyday activities is
what engineers do!

Cheryl is a licensed engineer in ten states, including her home
state of Indiana. She recieved a Bachelor of Science degree
in Civil Engineering from Purdue University. She and her
husband own a civil engineering firm in Avon, Indiana.

As an educator, literacy advocate, and writer Judy (the
teacher) joined the team to create stories about
engineering for young children.

Judy received a Bachelor of Science degree in Early Childhood
Education from Georgia State University and a Master of
Science in Reading and Literacy from Walden University. She
currently resides in Woodstock, Georgia.

Judy's daughter, Jill VanMatre (the artist), captured
the essence of the stories with sketch, watercolor, and
technology.

Jill received her Bachelor of Science in Communications
with a minor in Drawing and Painting from Kennesaw
State University. She is a freelance photographer and
artist in Georgia.

I Can Find A Way! I'm Lucy Kay!
is the second book in a collection of stories,
I Can Be An Engineer, written for young children.

The first book, *Yes I Can! I'm Clover Anne!*
can be purchased on Amazon.com.

www.icanbeanengineer.com

You can

Ride your  , walk your , watch ,

play video games, your mom, to visit

grandma, take a to school, drink clean

water, take a , flush the , have clean

, play on the , go to the ,

listen to , turn on a , eat an , work

on your , have lights in your , play

at night, with your friends,

and read this book...

...thanks to an Engineer!

Also from the
I Can Be An Engineer Series:

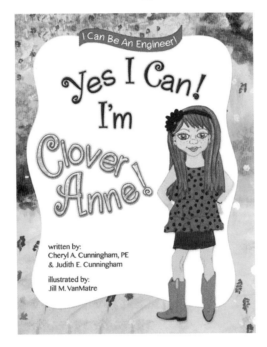

available on Amazon.com

Coming Soon!

Ziva Marie
The next character in the series,
"I Can Be An Engineer."

Made in the USA
Lexington, KY
29 July 2015